THE BABY GARDEN

Jennifer Bosma

Ambassador International
GREENVILLE, SOUTH CAROLINA & BELFAST, NORTHERN IRELAND

www.ambassador-international.com

The Baby Garden

Illustrated by Windha Sukmanindya

Hardback ISBN: 978-1-62020-447-4
Paperback ISBN: 978-1-62020-928-8
eISBN: 978-1-62020-944-8

Page Layout by Hannah Nichols
Ebook Conversion by Anna Riebe Raats

AMBASSADOR INTERNATIONAL
Emerald House
411 University Ridge, Suite B14
Greenville, SC 29601, USA
www.ambassador-international.com

AMBASSADOR BOOKS
The Mount
2 Woodstock Link
Belfast, BT6 8DD, Northern Ireland, UK
www.ambassadormedia.co.uk

The colophon is a trademark of Ambassador, a Christian publishing company.

Dedicated to my Dad, AJ Richter, who I miss tremendously, but now has the pleasure of meeting my future grandkids as a frequent visitor to The Baby Garden.

"Before I formed you in the womb I knew you."

–Jeremiah 1:5

I have a very big secret to share.

It is important to tell it before I get older because after that, I will forget.

Jesus designs it this way so we trust and have faith only in Him.

Up in God's glorious heaven, far, far away there is a wonderful place.

It is reserved just for God's little people. I know all about it because this is where I lived before coming to Earth. In fact, so did you and everybody else. It's called the Baby Garden.

The Baby Garden is the prettiest place that I have ever seen. There is a big castle, streaming with ivy and colorful flowers. The sky is always blue and the ground is sprinkled with big, fluffy pillows of white.

There are baby boys and girls of every race and color.

Each has their own special God-given talent that they practice in the garden.

Every baby has two heavenly friends.
They are called Guardian Angels.

God tells the angels to always guide and protect their child.

Heaven is also where God's son, Jesus lives. Everyone in the Baby Garden loves spending time with Him. You can talk to Jesus and ask Him anything.

Sometimes while talking, He tells babies about their parents, who are waiting for them on Earth. The babies get very excited to meet their new Mommies and Daddies.

Jesus knows exactly where we will live and what our lives will be like when we grow up. The talents we practiced in heaven will be very useful to us throughout our lives on Earth.

Before leaving the Baby Garden, our angels promise us that they will never leave us. They tell us to trust Jesus for our protection and remind us that the only way to return to heaven is by asking Jesus into our hearts. He is the only one with the key and the directions.

Then the angels show us a very important book. That book is called the Bible. The Bible will guide us towards Jesus' perfect plan for our lives. It is important to read this every day to be reminded of God's promises.

Finally, Jesus decides that it is time for me to leave the Baby Garden. He sends me to a warm and cozy place inside my mommy's tummy. I shrink in size and begin to grow all over again. I love watching and feeling the changes that happen to me every day.

My mommy and daddy talk to me all the time.
Sometimes my mommy will sing songs that
sound like the angels in heaven.

I hear them pray over me, asking for my protection and happiness.

After a while, I become snuggled very tightly inside my mommy. I know the time has come to leave this cozy spot. There is a bright light and I am moving towards it!

Suddenly, I am face to face with my mommy and daddy. They have bright smiles and even tears in their eyes. Jesus has chosen such wonderful parents for me! I am so content being with them now. Life is such an exciting adventure, growing and learning each and every day!

Someday I will return to heaven. For now, I am ready to live a long life here on Earth, serving Jesus. It is my prayer that I stay on the path He has designed for me, that will lead me back to His glorious heaven for eternity.

"For He shall give His angels charge
over you, to keep you in all your ways."

–Psalm 91:11

About the Author

Jennifer Bosma has an enthusiasm for life and embraces the joy in each day. She has been married for 30 years and has three grown daughters and one granddaughter. Enjoying quality family time is a passion for her.

Jennifer is a 3rd grade teacher known for interjecting fun into her classroom where she strives to instill a love of learning in her students. She loves to travel, explore new places, and enjoy the great outdoors. Bible studies and weekly church time keep her grounded in her faith. She and her husband reside in Marietta, Georgia.

For more information about
The Baby Garden
please visit:
www.jenniferbosma.com
www.facebook.com/jenniferjbosma
www.instagram.com/jennifer.bosma

For more information about
AMBASSADOR INTERNATIONAL
please visit:
www.ambassador-international.com
@AmbassadorIntl
www.facebook.com/AmbassadorIntl